My Angel

By Dwayne Johnson

My Angel

DWAYNE JOHNSON

ILLUSTRATIONS BY

OLIVIA COLEMAN

COPYRIGHTS PAGE

About the Author

I was born in Jamaica on 7 April 1986. I grew up with my mother and her side of the family, because I never knew my father or his side of the family. Growing up I had 1 older brother, 2 younger brothers, and 1 sister. We lived in a small 2-bedroom house in a small community called Hellshire Park in Portmore, Jamaica.

As a child, growing up was fun and challenging at the same time. We barely had any food - if I was at school with no lunch then one of my friends would share what they had with me. I was always playing outside, as at the time this is all the fun in the world – but I was always closely watching the shoes on my feet, making sure they were okay because if they became worn out I would not be able to get a new pair until December as a Christmas gift from my grandmother in England.

I remember vividly when my mother came to me and my brother, telling us that she and my little sister would be leaving us for a while to go to England. I was so scared - I was just 11 years old, and my brother was 13 years old.

2 years later we migrated to England. Arriving at Heathrow Airport with my brother was a dream come true. We were with our mother and family again.

A few years later, my big brother passed away in a motoring accident. At this point, I didn't know how I survived.

A few years later I got married and started my own family. Now, at 35 years old, I am divorced with 2 children - my daughter Tehillah and my son Nemiah Johnson. Determined and guided by my life experiences, I am fully focused on moving forward. Stay on this journey with me.

Susan was the only child of Carmen and Hector Johnson. The family moved into their new home with Poochie, their cat.

Only to find a puppy in the basement. The Johnson's knew that the previous owners of the house moved to another country.

They believed that the old owners must have left the puppy behind. Susan begged her parents to let her keep the puppy, promising to look after it. They agreed.

On her way to her new school the next day, with her heavy rucksack on her back and her shoes pinching her toes,

all Susan could think about was her new pet and what she was going to name it.

After school had finished, Susan took the puppy to the park. The puppy would not leave her side the whole time they were there or indeed until Susan had left for school the next morning.
The two of them had become very close very quickly.

Since starting at the new school, Susan had been very quiet. At lesson time she would find a seat in the furthest corner of the classroom, and she never spoke to anyone in her class. She even chose to stay inside during playtimes.

Carmen and Hector were worried, as Susan's grades were low. They made a call to the school, and a home visit was arranged.

When Susan's teacher, Mrs Graham, made the visit to the Johnsons' home, she was surprised to see that Susan was seemingly very happy. Susan was smiling while playing with her puppy. She joined in conversation with the adults.

"Susan is relaxed and happy when she is with the puppy," Carmen responded. "She has been a real angel to Susan. Susan used to stutter, but we have not heard her stutter once since we found the puppy."

"That's wonderful," said Mrs Graham.

"That's it, Mum! I will call her Angel because she is my angel," Susan said enthusiastically.

Mrs Graham said, "That's a lovely name. I think that in this very special circumstance I am going to make the unusual decision to allow you to bring your puppy – I mean Angel – to school. It's Toy Day on Friday, and you could bring her in instead of a toy. Would you like that, Susan?"

"Yes, Mrs Graham, I would like that very much," said Susan.

When Susan returned to school the next day, in her excitement she spoke to a girl, Kera, whom she had never spoken to before. "I am going to bring my puppy, Angel, to school on Friday," said Susan.

"I can't wait to meet her," Kera responded. "This is the first time anyone has ever spoken to me. I will have to thank Angel for that!"
"I hadn't noticed that you are always on your own. I am always by myself too," Susan said.
"Friends, yeah?" asked Kera. "Friends," Susan agreed.

For the rest of the week Susan made sure that she paid attention in class and did her homework every night.

Friday came. The class was excited at the arrival of the dog but knew that they had to sit still and stay quiet. Angel walked to each child's desk and gave each girl or boy a look and a sniff. Then she sat in front of the class to watch them all work. Mrs Graham noticed that the class was very well behaved – concentrating and listening. Angel had made them pay attention, and all the students did their best work that day.

Susan was allowed to bring Angel to school every Friday, and now everyone in the class did his or her homework every night, excited about Fridays. Susan now had many friends in her class, as well as a best friend – Kera. Her grades improved, and she no longer stuttered at school. Mrs Graham asked Susan if she thought she would be able to speak in a school assembly. Susan agreed, saying, "Angel gives me the confidence to do anything."

Susan and Angel were waiting in the
wings of the assembly hall. She could
hear the voices and feet of the children
piling into the hall, class by class, in
single file. She began getting nervous.
She could feel her legs begin to wobble.

Then she felt Angel rub her head gently against her leg, and she saw her puppy give her a loving look. Susan stood up straight, held her head high and waited for her introduction.

"I would like to introduce to you, my angel. I found Angel, lonely and cold, with no food. Her eyes lit up when she saw me. She needed lots of love and care that I wanted to give. We have been together ever since. She taught me how to be proud of myself, to work hard, to improve my grades and that practice makes perfect.

She showed me that sharing is good, and I shared her with my class. They are happy that they met her, and they love her. Everybody looks forward to coming to class. She helped me find my best friend, and most of all, I no longer stutter! So please meet Angel – my angel."

THE END

THANK YOU

I want to thank a few people that has help me towards this journey, I am for ever in dept.

The Most-high, the almighty God I want to thank you publicly, you have never leave me nor forsake me, You're the king.

I want to thank my 2 children Tehillah and Nemiah Johnson you are my greatest blessing and I love you both endlessly.

I want to thank my mother Ann Marie for never giving up on me in the hardest of times, thank you mum I love you.

My grandmother, Leila aka MAMA R.I.P to the greatest grandmother. I thank you

RIP to my big brother Shuane, this is a proud moment.

My god children's you can do anything you put your mind too (Lashaun, Ayana, Micah, Zayda-sky and Rai'jurnai.
I love Ya'll.
The illustrator Olivia Coleman thank you, you're so talented.

For the once that support me you are now my family, I truly appreciate you and thank you from the bottom of my heart, let's stay on this journey together.

Printed in Great Britain
by Amazon